This book belongs to

....

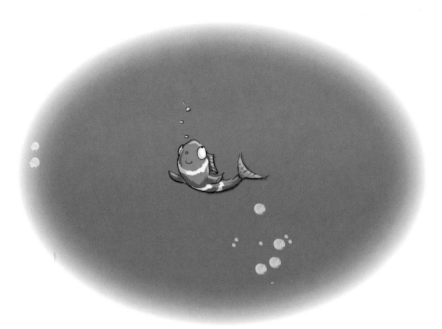

Quarto is the authority on a wide range of topics.

Quarto educates, entertains and enriches the lives of
our readers—enthusiasts and lovers of hands-on living.

www.quartoknows.com

© 2019 Quarto Publishing plc

First published in 2019 by QEB Publishing,
an imprint of The Quarto Group.
6 Orchard Road, Suite 100
Lake Forest, CA 92630
T: +1 949 380 7510
F: +1 949 380 7575
www.QuartoKnows.com

A CIP record for this book is available from the Library
of Congress.

ISBN 978-0-7112-4937-0

Based on the original story by A. H. Benjamin and
Bill Bolton
Author of adapted text: Katie Woolley
Series Editor: Joyce Bentley
Series Designer: Sarah Peden

Manufactured in Guangdong, China TT012020
9 8 7 6 5 4 3 2 1

MIX
Paper from
responsible sources
FSC® C016973

Shark lives in a sunken ship at the bottom of the sea.

He is lonely all by himself.

"I just want some friends," says Shark.

One day, Shark has an idea. He heads out to find some friends.

Octopus swims by. He has long arms that go splish, splash, splosh!

"Got you!" shouts Shark. He puts Octopus in a bag.

Shark hides in the seaweed.

Lobster comes along. His claws go
click, clack, clickety-clack!

"Got you!" snaps Shark. He puts Lobster in the bag, too.

"Oh, no!" cries Lobster.

Shark hides inside
a dark cave.

It's not long until
Turtle swims past.
His flippers go flip,
flap, flop!

Shark leaps out of the cave!

"Got you!" he laughs. He puts Turtle in the bag.

Just then, Jellyfish wobbles past.
Swish, swash, swoosh!

Shark pounces out from behind
the sand!

"Got you, too!" he says.

"Let me out!" shouts Jellyfish.

Shark's bag is getting very full!

Shark is having such fun. He wants to find more friends. He hides in a deep hole.

Starfish crawls past the hole. Shark jumps out and stuffs Starfish into the bag, too.

"Time to go home," says Shark. "I'm hungry!"

Octopus, Lobster, Turtle, Jellyfish, and Starfish are all in Shark's bag.

"Shark is going to eat us for lunch," cries Jellyfish.

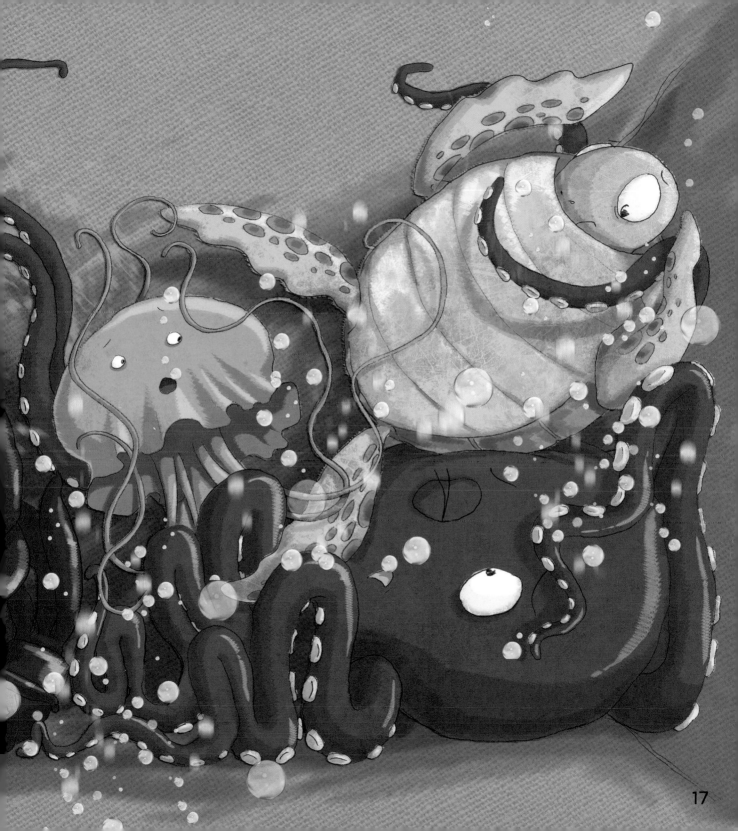

Back inside the sunken ship,
Shark opens the bag.

"Hello, everyone!" he says.
"Welcome to my home!"

"Please don't eat us for lunch!" shouts Lobster.
Shark goes into the kitchen.

"Surprise!" shouts Shark. "I made a cake for you all!"

"It looks delicious!" says Turtle.

"I like cake," says Lobster.

"Next time you want us to come over for cake, you can just ask!" says Octopus.

So, Shark did!

Story Words

bag

cake

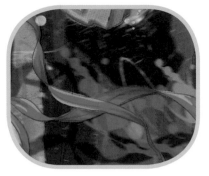

cave

hole

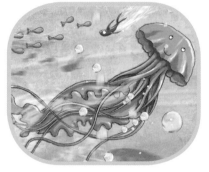

Jellyfish

Lobster

Octopus

sand

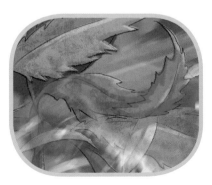

seaweed

Shark

ship

Starfish

Turtle

Let's Talk About Shark Wants a Friend

Look carefully at the book cover.

Who can you see in the picture?

What do you think each of the characters is feeling?

Lots of creatures live in the sea.

Can you remember which animals are in this story?

Do you have a favorite?

The animals are all trapped in Shark's bag.

Look at their faces. How are they feeling?

How do you think Shark is feeling?

Do you think Shark goes about making friends in the right way?

What other ways could he have tried to make friends?

What happens at the end of the story?

Did you like the ending?

Fun and Games

Sound out the letters, and read the words.
Find the objects in the big picture.

fish   sea   shell   coins   teeth
chair   seaweed   bubbles

Choose the correct word to complete these sentences.

ship   bag   hides   cake

Shark lives in a sunken .... at the bottom of the sea.

He puts Octopus in a ....

Next, Shark .... in the seaweed.

"I made a .... for you all!"

Your Turn

Now that you have read the story,
try telling it in your own words.
Use the pictures below to help you.

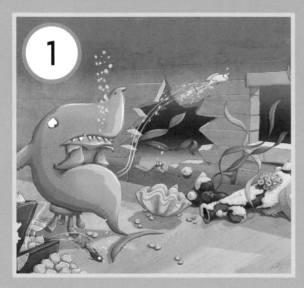

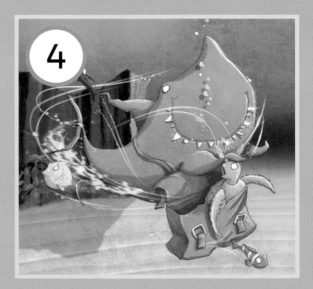

READING TOGETHER

- When reading this book together, suggest that your child looks at the pictures to help them make sense of any words they are unsure about, and ask them to point to any letters they recognize.

- Try asking questions such as, "Can you break the word into parts?" and "Are there clues in the picture that help you?"

- During the story, ask your child questions such as, "Can you remember what has happened so far?" and "What do you think will happen next?"

- Look at the story words on pages 24–25 together. Encourage your child to find the pictures and the words on the story pages, too.

- There are lots of activities you can play at home with your child to help them with their reading. Write the alphabet onto 26 cards, and hide them around the house. Encourage your child to shout out the letter name when they find a card!

- In the car, play "I Spy" to help your child learn to recognize the first sound in a word.

- Organize a family read-aloud session once a week! Each family member chooses something to read out loud. It could be their favorite book, a magazine, a menu, or the back of a food package.

- Give your child lots of praise, and take great delight when your child successfully sounds out a new word.

Level 3

"It looks delicious!" says Turtle.
"I like cake," says Lobster.

"Next time you want us to come over for cake, you can just ask!" says Octopus.
So Shark did!

Longer sentences ✓

Varied language ✓

Wider vocabulary ✓

Pictures and words support each other ✓